THREE DOLLAR MULE

THREE DOLLAR MULE

by Clyde Robert Bulla

illustrated by Paul Lantz

little rainbow ®

Troll Associates

To Amanda and Levi

Copyright © 1960 by Clyde Robert Bulla.
Copyright © renewed 1988 by Clyde Robert Bulla.

Published by Troll Associates, Inc.
Little Rainbow is a trademark of Troll Associates.

All rights reserved. No part of this book may be reproduced or utilized
in any form or by any means, electronic or mechanical, including
photocopying, recording, or by any information storage and retrieval system,
without written permission from the publisher.

Printed in the United States of America.

10   9   8   7   6   5   4   3   2

Library of Congress Cataloging-in-Publication
Bulla, Clyde Robert.
Three dollar mule / by Clyde Robert Bulla; illustrated by Paul Lantz.
p.   cm.
Summary: A boy finds himself the owner of a mule that likes children
but is very hostile to adults. To the parents' dismay and the boy's delight,
all attempts to sell the animal fail.
ISBN 0-8167-3711-8 (lib.)   ISBN 0-8167-3598-0 (pbk.)
[1. Mules—Fiction.]   I. Lantz, Paul, (date)-   ill.
PZ7.B912TH   1994
[FIC]—dc20   94-18508

Contents

1. Bar-B Ranch

The day was warm for October. The sun was hot on the boy's head.

He was working in the garden back of the ranch house. He was raking up dead leaves and vines.

A woman came out of the house. "Why don't you rest a while?" she said.

"I'm nearly through," said the boy. He raked up the last of the tomato vines. "There! How does it look?"

"It never looked better," she said. "Come on up to the house, Don. There's a piece of apple pie for you."

"Thank you, Mrs. Hibbs," he said, "but I'd better go. I want to get home before dark."

"You'll have enough time," she said.

"But I want to stop on the way," he said. "I want to stop at the Bar-B Ranch."

"Oh," said Mrs. Hibbs. "You want to see your horse."

"He isn't mine," said Don.

"He will be, won't he?" she asked.

"I hope so," said Don.

"You hope so?" she said. "I thought it was a sure thing."

"No, it isn't a sure thing," he said.

"You'll be twelve next month, won't you?" said Mrs. Hibbs. "And didn't your father say you could have a horse when you were twelve?"

"All he says is *maybe*," said Don. "He says he wants to be sure I'm ready for a horse of my own."

"I think you're ready," she said.

"So do I," said Don. "I know how to take care of a horse. And I've been working and saving money for a year so I can help buy the one I want."

"Maybe this will help." Mrs. Hibbs took some money out of her pocket and gave it to him.

Don said, "It's three dollars!"

"It isn't too much," she said. "I'm glad to have this garden cleaned off. Mr. Hibbs can't do much until his stiff neck gets better. Come back next Saturday, and maybe I'll have some more work for you."

Don thanked her. He said good-by and started down the mountain.

He saw his sister, Jenny, in the road far
below. He knew her by her bright blue
sweater.

Don began to run. He took short cuts.
He slid down into the road.

"I wish you wouldn't run so fast," said
Jenny. "You might hurt your leg again."

Last winter Don had fallen on the ice
and broken his leg. Sometimes the leg still

hurt. It hurt just a little now, but he said nothing about it to Jenny.

"Did you come to walk home with me?" he asked.

She nodded. "I've been waiting down here."

"Why didn't you come on up the mountain?" he asked.

"It was so nice here under the trees," she said, "and I had a book to read."

Jenny was the family bookworm. She was almost two years younger than Don, but she had read as many books as he had.

"I'm reading a good one now," she said. "It's *Arabian Nights.*"

They walked along together. The money jingled in Don's pocket.

"Mrs. Hibbs paid me three dollars," he said.

"Oh, that's good," said Jenny. "You might have enough to buy your horse, even if Father doesn't help you."

"No," said Don. "Ben Gold is a thoroughbred, and thoroughbreds cost a lot of money."

"I think Father is going to help you," said Jenny. "I heard him say he was glad

you wanted a thoroughbred horse. He says that's the only kind to have. He says he wouldn't have an animal on our ranch that he couldn't be proud of."

"I'd be proud of Ben Gold if I had him," said Don, "but I don't want him just because he's a thoroughbred. I want him because I like him."

Bar-B Ranch was just ahead. Jim Crane was there to open the gate for them.

Jim Crane owned Bar-B Ranch. It was not a large ranch, but it was known all over the West. It was known for its fine horses.

"Do you want to see your favorite horse?" asked Jim. "If you do, you know where to find him."

Don and Jenny went past the stables and out to the pasture.

"There he is!" said Jenny.

Ben Gold was eating grass near the pasture gate. He was a slim horse, with long, slim legs. His color was bay—a light brown that looked gold in the sun.

When he saw Don and Jenny he gave his head a shake. He started to run away. Then he stopped and looked back at them.

"He wants to play," said Jenny.

"Come back, Ben Gold," said Don.

The horse came back and put his head over the fence. Don patted his neck. Jenny ran her fingers through his mane.

"Ben Gold, you're coming to live with us," she said.

"I wish I could be sure of that," said Don. "I wish Father would *tell* me!"

"Maybe he wants to surprise you on your birthday," said Jenny. "Maybe that's why he doesn't tell you."

The sun was low over the mountains.

"Let's go," said Don. "We have to get home before dark."

They left Ben Gold. They said good-by

to Jim Crane and went on down the road.

They had gone a little way when Don asked, "Do you hear that sound?"

"Yes," she said. "What is it?"

"I don't know," he said. "It sounds like someone beating a rug."

They walked faster. The sound grew louder—*thud, thud, thud!*

There was a bend in the road ahead. Just around the bend they stopped. Jenny cried out.

By the side of the road was a wagon. Two old horses were hitched to it. Three or four other horses were tied to the back of the wagon.

Near the wagon was a mule. He was tied with his nose against a tree.

A man stood under the tree. His face was red. His hair had fallen over his eyes. With a long, heavy stick held in both his hands, he was beating the mule.

2. Sinbad

Don ran forward.

"Stop that!" he shouted.

The man dropped the stick. There was a wild look in his eyes.

The mule humped his back. He kicked at the man.

The man picked up the stick.

"Don't you hit him again," said Don.

"Didn't you see him?" said the man. "He tried to kick me."

"I should think he would," said Don.

"You ought to be ashamed," said Jenny.

"You think I ought to be ashamed, do you?" The man sat down on a rock. He looked very tired. "You think I'm a mean old man for beating this poor mule. Let me tell you something. You ought to feel sorry for *me*. I'm a horse trader, and I don't go around being mean to animals, but this mule—! I've had him two days, and it seems like two years. He hates me."

"If he hates you, there must be a reason," said Don.

"He hates the whole world," said the man. "When I first got him, I tied him to the wagon and led him along, and he was like any other mule. Then he started to

pull back. He kicked me into a ditch. If I went near him, he tried to bite me." The man's voice shook. He looked as if he were about to cry. "Just now he kicked a hole in my wagon. What are you going to do with an animal like that?"

The mule laid back his ears and showed his teeth.

"There! Did you see that look he gave me?" The man got to his feet. "I'll show him!"

"If you feel that way, what do you keep him for?" asked Don.

"Because I can't get rid of him, that's why. Who would want such a mule?" The man looked at Don. "Maybe you'd like to buy him."

"I would if I could," said Don, "but—"

"How much money have you got?" asked the man.

"I don't know for sure," said Don. "It's in the bank."

"I mean, how much have you got in your pocket right now?" asked the man.

"Three dollars," said Don.

"Let's see it."

Don showed him the money. The man took it. He counted it.

"Shake hands?" he asked.

Don shook hands with him.

"Boy," said the man, "you've bought yourself a mule."

He jumped into the wagon.

"Wait," said Don.

The man did not answer. He whipped the horses and drove away.

Don and Jenny looked after the wagon until it was out of sight.

Jenny asked, "Did you buy the mule—really?"

"He said so. We shook hands on it," said Don.

"And that means you bought him?" she asked.

"It's what men do when they make a deal," said Don. "They shake hands so neither one can back out."

"I'm glad you bought him," said Jenny. "That man will never whip him any more."

They looked at the mule. He was mostly gray, the color of mud. His nose was white, as if he had dipped it in flour. One ear stood up and one hung down.

"He isn't very pretty," said Don.

"He looks like a sad clown," said Jenny.

She went toward the mule. Don pulled her back.

"Be careful," he said. "We'd better go get Father."

"He isn't home," she said. "He went to the city to sell a load of cattle."

"If this mule is as bad as the man said, we'll have to keep him tied up," said Don.

"He doesn't look the same since the man went away," said Jenny.

It was true. The ugly look was gone from the mule's eyes. He was watching them.

"He's tied so close to the tree, he can't move his head," said Don. He untied the rope. He let it out a few feet and tied it again.

"That's better, isn't it, mule?" he said.

"We can't go on calling him 'mule,'"

said Jenny. "Let's give him a name. I know a good one."

"What is it?" asked Don.

"Sinbad," she said. "It's out of the book I'm reading."

"Sinbad was a sailor," said Don. "This mule never sailed anywhere."

"But Sinbad had a lot of trouble," said Jenny, "and this mule has had trouble, too."

It was growing dark.

"We'd better go," said Don.

"And leave Sinbad here?" said Jenny.

"Maybe I could lead him," said Don. "He's quiet now. I don't believe he's as wild as that man said."

"Neither do I," said Jenny. "I'm not afraid."

"I'm not afraid, either," said Don, "but let's be careful. You get behind that rock, and I'll stay behind the tree while I untie him."

Jenny stood behind the rock. Don stayed behind the tree and untied the rope.

He gave a little pull on the rope. The mule took a step toward him.

Don pulled on the rope again. The mule took another step.

"He's going to lead!" said Don.

"He's not wild at all," said Jenny. "Come on, Sinbad."

And she and Don led the mule down the road.

3. A Noise at Daybreak

It was almost dark when they led the mule up to the gate at home. The ranch house windows were bright with lights. Mother was in the doorway.

"Don? Jenny?" she called.

"Yes, Mother," they called back. Jenny opened the gate and Don led Sinbad through.

"Where have you been?" asked Mother. "Why didn't you—?" She stopped. "What is that?"

"It's a friend we brought to supper," said Jenny.

"Don't joke about this," said Mother. "Where did you get that mule!"

"He's mine," said Don.

He and Jenny told her what had happened.

"His name is Sinbad," said Jenny. "See? He lets me pet him."

"We'll talk about this later," said Mother. "Come in and eat your supper."

"I'd like to take care of Sinbad first," said Don.

"All right," said Mother, "but don't be long."

Don took Sinbad to the water tank and waited while he drank. He led him into the box stall in the barn.

"I won't have to tie you up in here," said Don. "You can lie down if you want to."

He threw some hay into the stall before he went to the house.

Mother and Jenny were waiting at the supper table. Mother was so quiet that Don asked her, "Is something the matter? Are you sorry I bought the mule?"

"I don't know," she said. "I just don't know what your father will say."

After supper she sent them to bed.

"Can't we wait up for Father?" asked Don.

"No, he may be late," she said. "You can talk to him in the morning."

Don tried to stay awake. He lay in bed and listened for his father's car, but he was asleep before his father came home.

Early in the morning he woke. There was a noise in his ears as loud as a train whistle: "E-e-e-e-onk! E-e-e-e-onk, onk onk!"

He jumped out of bed.

Jenny ran into the room.

"Did you hear it, too?" he asked.

"Yes," she said.

They looked out the window toward the barn. The bottom door of the box stall was shut, but the top door was open. Sinbad's head was in the doorway.

"It was Sinbad," said Jenny. "He was braying."

"Onk!" went the mule. "Onk, onk!"

"I've got to stop him," said Don. "He's going to wake everybody up."

He put on his shoes and ran out of the room. Outside the door he met his father.

"I thought I heard a noise," said Father. He was half dressed and half awake. "Maybe I was dreaming. Did you hear anything?"

"It was Sinbad," said Don.

"What?" said Father.

"Didn't Mother tell you about the mule?" asked Don.

"What mule?" asked Father.

Sinbad was braying again.

"I'll try to stop him." Don ran out to the barn. "Sinbad, don't do that!" he shouted. "What's the matter with you?"

He threw some hay into the box stall. Sinbad began to eat.

Don's father had come out to the barn. He was wide awake now. He said, "I think you'd better tell me what all this is about."

"All right," said Don. "I didn't have a chance before."

He told his father about Sinbad and the man who had sold him.

"You didn't *buy* this animal!" said Father.

"Yes, I did," said Don.

"It must be a joke." Father looked into the barn at Sinbad. "No one would sell a mule for three dollars—even a mule as ugly as this."

"He did sell him," said Don.

"Then there's something wrong with the mule and the man, too," said Father. "Come on. Let's have some breakfast. Then we're going to find out what this is all about."

After breakfast Don and his father got into the car. They drove up the road.

"Where did you first see the mule?" asked Father.

Don showed him the place. "He was tied to that tree. The man was whipping him."

"Did you see the man leave?" asked Father.

"Yes," said Don. "He was in his wagon. He went the same way we are going."

"We'll find him then," said Father. "He hasn't had time to get far."

They drove past Bar-B Ranch and on around the foot of the mountain. They came to the bridge over Blue River.

On the river bank, just off the road, was a campfire. A man was sitting near it. He was eating out of a tin dish. Behind him were several horses tied to a wagon.

"That's the man," said Don.

Father stopped the car. He and Don got out. The man looked surprised to see them.

"My boy brought home a mule yesterday," said Father. "He says you sold it to him for three dollars. I know it must have been a mistake."

"It was no mistake," said the man. "I sold the mule to your boy. We made a deal and shook hands on it, didn't we?" he asked Don.

"Yes," said Don.

"But we don't need a mule," said Father. "We don't *want* a mule."

"You've got one, just the same. I wouldn't take him back if you paid me."

The man washed his tin dish in the river. He stamped on the fire to put it out. He hitched two of his horses to the wagon and tied the other three behind. "If you don't want that mule," he said, as he got into the wagon, "you can get rid of him the same way I did."

He shook his whip at the horses and drove away.

4. *Sinbad and the Cattle*

Father said, on the way home, "So you really bought this mule."

"Yes, I did," said Don.

"We've always been proud of the animals on our ranch," said Father. "All the cattle come from the best stock. Even our chickens and ducks and geese are from the best stock we can buy. Do you think our ranch is any place for a three dollar mule?"

Don was quiet. He did not know what to say.

Father said, when they were home again, "You bought this mule without thinking. I want you to think now. I want you to make up your mind what you are going to do about him."

He went into the house.

Don walked slowly out to the barn. Jenny was there, by the box-stall door.

"Father doesn't like what I did," said Don.

"Why not?" asked Jenny.

"He thinks we can't be proud of a mule like Sinbad," said Don.

They looked into the stall. Sinbad was standing with his head down. His eyes were half shut. There was straw in his tail.

"If we brushed him, he might look better," said Jenny.

"Let's not brush him yet. His back is sore where the man whipped him," said Don.

"Poor old Sinbad." Jenny asked Don, "Did Father say you couldn't keep him?"

"No, but he doesn't like the idea of a mule on the ranch."

"I don't see why," said Jenny. "There are things Sinbad could do to help."

"He could pull the little plow and plow gardens in the spring," said Don.

"He could pull the little wagon, too," she said.

"Yes, or the sled," said Don. "We could hitch him to the wagon or the sled and haul wood from the timber."

"Let's make a list of all the things he can do to help," said Jenny, "and then show the list to Father."

"But we don't know Sinbad can do these

things yet," said Don.

"Let's try him," she said.

"I don't want to put a harness on him now," said Don. "It would hurt his sore back."

"I wish he didn't have to stay in the barn all the time," said Jenny. "His back would get well faster if he could be out in the sun and fresh air."

"He doesn't have to stay in the barn all day," said Don.

He put a rope on Sinbad's halter and led him outside. Jenny helped lead him to the pasture. It was the pasture where the cattle were.

Sinbad's ears stood up straight.

"He likes it here," said Jenny.

"I'm going to leave him for a while," said Don. "He can eat grass, and he won't hurt anything."

Don untied the halter rope and turned Sinbad loose.

The first thing the mule did was to lie
down and roll. Then he got up and began
to run. He ran in a circle, with his head low.

Far across the pasture, the cattle stopped
eating grass. They stood still, with their
heads lifted.

Sinbad came close to them. They began
to run. Down the pasture hill they ran, with

the mule behind them.

"Sinbad!" shouted Don.

Father and Mother came out of the house.

"Stop him!" said Father.

The calves were bawling. The cattle ran into one another. One of the cows fell down.

"I'll have to rope that mule!" Father ran toward the barn. But before he could get there, Sinbad had stopped running.

He trotted back to the gate. He let Don put the rope on his halter.

"See what happens with an animal like that around!" said Father. "Some of my best cattle might have been hurt."

"He didn't mean to hurt them," said Don. "He was just running because he felt good."

Father did not answer. He turned and walked away, as if he were too angry to talk.

5. A Story

Back in the barn, Sinbad was quiet. Don sat
on the manger of the box stall. The mule
came close to him.

"Oh, yes, you're good now!" said Don.
"But why can't you be good when I want you
to be? How am I going to help you when

you run after the cattle and act like a wild mule?"

Jenny came into the barn. "Were you talking to someone?" she asked.

"I was talking to Sinbad," said Don, "but I don't know why. It doesn't do any good to talk to him."

Jenny climbed up on the manger. She sat down beside Don. "I've been thinking about something," she said.

"What?" he asked.

"It's something I read," she said. "It's a story about a man who could tame horses. He could tame the wildest horse in the country. Do you want to know how?"

"Is this a true story?" asked Don.

"I can't remember," she said, "but in the book this is how he did it. He whispered and told the horse what he wanted it to do."

"He *whispered*?" said Don.

"Yes. And, while he whispered, he

believed the horse could understand him. He believed so hard that the horse *did* understand him."

"I don't think that ever happened," said Don.

"You could try it," said Jenny.

"I don't know how," he said. "I don't know how to believe that hard. Anyway, that was for horses. It might not work with a mule." He rubbed Sinbad's ears. The mule closed his eyes as if he had gone to sleep.

"He's funny," said Jenny.

"Father doesn't think he's funny," said Don.

"No," said Jenny. "Father is going to talk to you about him. I heard him say so."

Mother called them to supper.

No one said much at the table. After supper Mother and Jenny began to wash and dry the dishes. Don and his father went into the living room.

Don asked, "Are the cattle all right?"

"Yes, as far as I can see," said Father.

"I'm sorry Sinbad scared them," said Don. "I won't let him into the pasture any more."

"You still want to keep this mule?" asked Father.

"Yes, if I can," said Don.

"Why?" asked his father.

"Well—I like him," said Don.

"You might like an elephant in the zoo," said Father, "but you wouldn't bring it home with you."

"An elephant doesn't belong on a ranch," said Don. "A mule does."

"What makes you think a mule belongs on this ranch?" asked Father.

Don said slowly, "Do you mean I can't keep Sinbad?"

"I mean that I want you to think about it," said Father. "I want you to give me one good reason why we should keep that mule on the ranch. If you can't do that, there's no use keeping him, is there?"

Don said nothing.

"Think about it for a while," said Father. "If you really think, you'll know the right thing to do."

He was smiling. He was not angry now. Don went to bed feeling better.

And the next morning Father was angry again. It was because of Sinbad's braying.

Very early, before the sun was up, the honking sound woke everyone in the house.

"That's the worst noise I ever heard. I'm sick of it!" said Father. "Does he have to do that every morning?"

"Mules do, sometimes," said Don. "It's like a rooster crowing in the morning."

"I don't mind a rooster, but that mule is

something else," said Father, "and you'd
better do something about him!"

It was Monday morning. Don and
Jenny went out to the road to wait for the
school bus.

"What are you going to do?" she asked.

"I don't know yet," he said.

"Poor Sinbad," said Jenny.

"I don't think we can keep him much
longer," said Don.

6. *Up the Mountain*

Don and Jenny went to school in Cotton-
wood Center, five miles from home. Don's
teacher was Mr. Pool.

At noon the teacher called Don up to his
desk. "You don't listen when I talk to you,"
he said. "I never saw you this way before."

"I'm sorry," said Don.

"You're not sick, are you?" asked Mr. Pool.

"No, sir," said Don.

"Is something the matter?" asked the teacher.

"Yes, sir," said Don.

"Do you want to tell me about it?" asked Mr. Pool.

Don told him about Sinbad. "He keeps getting into trouble with my father. And my father doesn't like mules, to begin with."

"Can't you find another place for Sinbad to live?" asked the teacher.

"I don't know," said Don.

"There must be people who would be glad to have him," said the teacher.

"Would you like to have him?" asked Don.

"My wife and I live in a trailer," said Mr. Pool. "I'm afraid there's no room for a mule. But what about your neighbors—the ones who live on ranches? Wouldn't one of them take him?"

"Maybe," said Don. "I could find out."

He and Jenny talked about it, as they rode home on the bus.

"Jim Crane wouldn't want Sinbad," said Don.

"We could go ask him today," said Jenny, "and see Ben Gold at the same time."

"No, Jim Crane has nothing but thoroughbred horses at Bar-B Ranch," said Don. "But what about the Hibbs Ranch?"

"Yes!" said Jenny. "Mr. Hibbs has a stiff neck, and he can't work hard. Sinbad could help him."

The bus driver let them out at home. They ran to the house.

Mother was in the kitchen.

"Is it too late for us to go up to the Hibbs Ranch?" asked Don. "We want to find out if Mr. Hibbs will take Sinbad."

Father came in off the back porch. "What's that?" he asked.

"We've been talking about what to do with Sinbad," said Don. "Maybe Mr. Hibbs would like to have him. Sinbad could help him plow gardens and haul wood."

Father looked pleased. "I can see you've been thinking."

"Mr. Pool helped me think," said Don.

"I like the idea," said Father. "Come on. I'll take you up the mountain."

He and Don and Jenny drove up to the Hibbs Ranch.

Mr. Hibbs came to the door. "Come in, come in!" he said.

"Stay to supper," said Mrs. Hibbs.

"Thank you, but we can't stay," said Father. "I just came up to bring Don and Jenny. They have something to say."

Don said, "Would you like to have a mule, Mr. Hibbs?"

Mr. Hibbs looked surprised. "Did you say a *mule?*"

"Yes," said Don. "We don't really need this mule on our ranch, and I thought you might like to have him."

"I—don't—know." Mr. Hibbs said to his wife, "Do we need a mule?"

"I never thought about it," she said.

"What kind is he?" asked Mr. Hibbs.

"Just a plain mule," said Jenny, "but he could help you with your work."

"It might be nice to have a mule," said Mr. Hibbs. "Of course, I'd have to see him first."

"You can see him now," said Father.

Mr. Hibbs put on his jacket and hat. His wife tied his red scarf around his neck. "You don't want to catch cold," she said.

Father and Mr. Hibbs got into the front seat of the car. Don and Jenny got into the back. They waved to Mrs. Hibbs and started down the mountain.

7. *The Water Tank*

They went to the corral in front of the
barn.

Don said, "We'll bring the mule out so
you can see him better."

Father and Mr. Hibbs waited by the
water tank. Don and Jenny went into the
box stall.

Sinbad touched Jenny's head with his
nose. He tried to lean against Don.

"He's glad to see us," said Jenny. She picked the straw off the mule's sides. "You have to look nice for Mr. Hibbs."

Don led the mule out of the barn.

"Well, well!" said Mr. Hibbs. "He's quite an animal. Is he gentle?"

"The man we bought him from said he was wild," said Don.

"But we don't think that man knew him very well," said Jenny.

"How old is he?" asked Mr. Hibbs.

"I don't know," said Don.

"I can look at his teeth and tell," said Mr. Hibbs. He tried to open Sinbad's mouth. "Now then—open up."

Sinbad shut his teeth together.

"Come on, open up." Mr. Hibbs was holding Sinbad by the nose.

Sinbad gave a snort. He struck Mr. Hibbs in the chest with his head. Mr. Hibbs' feet went into the air. There was a loud splash as he fell back into the water tank.

He went out of sight under the water. He came up sputtering and blowing.

Father pulled him out of the tank. Water poured from Mr. Hibbs' clothes.

"Into the house—quick!" said Father. He helped Mr. Hibbs across the corral.

Don looked at Sinbad. "See what you did, you—you *mule!*"

Mr. Hibbs' hat was floating in the tank. Jenny took it out. She shook the water off it.

"He liked you at first," Don said to Sinbad. "He doesn't like you now."

"Do you know what I think?" said Jenny. "I think Sinbad grew up where there were boys and girls and they were good to him. But men have been bad to him. That's why he's good with us and bad with men."

Don led Sinbad back to the box stall. "There," he said, as he shut the door, "you can't get into any more trouble for a while."

He and Jenny went to the house. Mr.

Hibbs was in a chair by the stove. He had a blanket around him.

"Are you all right, Mr. Hibbs?" asked Don.

"I d-d-don't know." Mr. Hibbs' teeth were chattering. "I'm so c-c-cold I can't tell!"

"Sinbad didn't mean to do it," said Jenny.

Father came out of the kitchen. He said to Mr. Hibbs, "I've hung your clothes out to dry. I'll get you some of mine to wear."

Mother brought a cup of hot tea. "Drink this, Mr. Hibbs," she said. "And please stay to supper."

"N-no, thank you," he said. "I want to get home. I want to get to bed."

Father took Mr. Hibbs home.

As soon as he came back, they had supper. Supper was their time to sit together and talk about what had happened that day. But this evening everyone was quiet.

Once Jenny spoke. "I don't suppose Mr. Hibbs wants Sinbad now."

Father said, "Would you want him if he pushed you into the water tank?"

And everyone was quiet again.

Just before they all went to bed, Father said, "We'd better get all the sleep we can, because, as soon as it's daylight, that mule will wake us up with his honking."

Don had an old alarm clock in his room. He set it for five o'clock. He put it under his pillow when he went to bed.

In the morning he woke at the first ring of the alarm. He put on his clothes and slipped out of the house.

The air was cold. There was only a little light in the sky. He went to the barn and let himself into the box stall.

He could see the mule standing in the half-darkness.

"Sinbad," he said, and the mule moved his head.

Don had come to the barn to keep the mule from braying. But now that he was here, he did not know how.

He thought, If he starts, what can I do? I can't hold his mouth shut.

Daylight was coming into the barn. When the stall grew light, it would be time for Sinbad to bray.

Don remembered something Jenny had said. It was about the man who had tamed horses by whispering in their ears.

He said to himself, I don't think it will work—not with Sinbad.

But he tried.

He pulled Sinbad's head down. He began to whisper into one of the long ears. He felt foolish, but he kept whispering.

"Sinbad," he said, "don't honk this morning. Father is asleep, and so are Mother and Jenny. If you honk, you'll wake them up. Don't wake them up, Sinbad."

Over and over he whispered it. Sinbad seemed to be listening.

The stall grew light. Sinbad opened his mouth once or twice, but he did not bray.

Don threw some hay into the manger. Sinbad began to eat.

Don went back to the house. His father and mother did not know he had been up. Jenny's room was next to his, and even she did not know.

Father said at breakfast, "That mule didn't wake us up, after all."

"Maybe he is getting to feel at home here," said Mother.

And Father said, as he looked at Don, "I hope he doesn't get to feeling *too* much at home."

8. *The Broken Door*

That evening after school Don and Jenny
went up the mountain to the Hibbs
Ranch. Mother had given them a glass of
grape jelly to take to Mr. Hibbs.

They found him out behind the house.
He was sawing wood.

"We were afraid you would be in bed," said Jenny.

"You didn't catch cold yesterday, did you?" asked Don.

"No, I didn't," said Mr. Hibbs, "and it's a funny thing, but the crick in my neck is gone."

"Did it go away when you fell in the water tank?" asked Jenny.

"I don't know," said Mr. Hibbs, "but I had that crick in my neck for years, and now it's gone."

"Maybe Sinbad made you well," said Jenny.

"Maybe," said Mr. Hibbs.

"Wouldn't you like to have him?" asked Don.

"No, no," Mr. Hibbs said quickly. "I'm glad I'm rid of the crick in my neck, but that mule might give me another one."

He sawed the last of the wood. Don

and Jenny helped him pile it up against the house. Then they started home.

On the way they stopped at Bar-B Ranch. Don had a lump of sugar for Ben Gold, and Jenny had brought an apple.

Ben Gold was in the pasture with the other horses. As soon as he saw Don and Jenny, he came trotting over to the fence.

He took the sugar first, then the apple. He took them gently and politely.

"He gets more beautiful all the time," said Jenny.

"He's getting his winter coat," said Don.

Jim Crane came out to the pasture.

"Having a look at your favorite horse?" he asked. "Are you going to take him home with you?"

"I'd like to," said Don.

"Maybe you can some day. I've been telling your father that Ben Gold is just the horse for you," said Jim Crane, "unless you like mules better."

"How did you know about Sinbad?" asked Don.

"Everybody around here knows about Sinbad," said Jim Crane.

"Would you like to have him?" asked Don. "If you want him, he won't cost you anything."

"No, I don't want a mule," said Jim Crane.

Jenny said, as she and Don went on toward home, "I don't care if we don't find a place for Sinbad. He's happy with us."

"Father isn't happy," said Don.

It was growing dark. They walked faster.

"Does your leg hurt?" she asked.

"How can you tell?" he asked.

"By the way you walk," she said.

"It doesn't hurt much," he said.

At the front gate they stopped. Sinbad was tied out in the corral.

"He was in the barn when we left," said Don. "What's he doing out there?"

Then they saw that the box-stall door was open. The bottom half of the door was gone.

Father came out of the house.

"Do you see what your mule did?" he asked.

"How did it happen?" asked Don.

Father told them how it had happened.

A chicken flew into the stall and did not know how to get out. It flapped its wings in Sinbad's face and frightened him. He wanted to get out of the stall, so he kicked the door down.

Once he was out of the barn, he jumped the corral fence into the pasture.

"He jumped that high fence?" said Don.

"He knocked off the top board," said Father.

"Did he get out with the cattle?" asked Don.

"Yes," said Father.

"He didn't run after them, did he?" asked Don.

"I didn't give him a chance," said Father. "I roped him and got him back into the corral."

"I'll fix the door of the box stall," said Don. "I'll fix the corral fence, too."

"You can fix them Saturday," said Father.

"All right," said Don.

"There's something else I want to say," said Father. "I don't like that mule around here. We might get up some morning and find he's kicked the barn down."

"If he can't stay in the barn or the pasture," said Don, "what shall I do with him?"

"You can take him out to the timber," said Father.

The timber was the part of the ranch that lay in the canyon of Blue River. It was half a mile from the house. The land was

rough and rocky. It was good for little
except the trees that grew there.

But grass grew among the trees. There
was pasture enough for Sinbad.

After supper Don led the mule down
the road. He had a lantern to light the way.

He led Sinbad into the timber. He left
him there under the trees.

Don woke early in the morning. The
room was just growing light. From a long
way off he heard a sound: "E-e-e-onk, onk,
onk!"

Alone in the timber Sinbad was braying.
It was a lonesome sound.

9. Mr. Holt

Days went by, and weeks. None of the neighbors wanted Sinbad. Don had asked them all.

One of them said, "I don't want that wild animal on my ranch." Another said, "I hear he tries to climb trees."

Someone had seen Sinbad with his front feet up against a tree.

"But he wasn't trying to climb it," Don said to Jenny. "He was reaching up to eat some little branches."

"Is he *that* hungry?" asked Jenny.

"He *likes* those little branches," said Don. "He has grass to eat, too."

"The grass is dead now," she said.

"It still has food in it. It's like hay," said Don. "And he can go to the river for water."

"Just the same, I know he doesn't like the timber," said Jenny. "He's too far from people."

They went to see him as often as they could. Every Saturday Don took him something—an apple or some sugar or salt. If Sinbad was not at the timber gate, he always came quickly when Don called.

Sometimes he leaned against Don as if he wanted to be as close to him as he could.

One Saturday Don and his father were mending a break in the pasture fence. They saw a car stop at the house. A man got out and came over to them.

They had never seen him before. He was not young and he was not very old. His arms were long and his neck was thick. He looked very strong.

His name was Holt, he said. "I live on a ranch east of town. I hear you've got a mule you don't need."

Father said, "You can talk to my boy about that."

The man asked Don, "Is he your mule?"

"Yes," said Don.

"Do you want me to take him off your hands?" asked the man.

"I—I don't know," said Don.

"You've been trying to give him away, haven't you?" asked the man.

"Yes," said Don.

"Show him the mule," said Father.

Don walked to the timber with Mr. Holt. Sinbad came out from among the trees.

"So that's the mule," said Mr. Holt. "They say he's a wild one."

"He isn't wild with my sister and me," said Don.

"He won't be wild with me for long," said the man. "I never saw a mule I couldn't break."

"How do you break them?" asked Don.

"I have my ways." The man took a few steps toward Sinbad.

The mule laid back his ears.

Mr. Holt stopped. He asked Don, "Shall I come and get him this afternoon?"

"I'm not ready to give him away," said Don.

"Oh," said Mr. Holt. "You want some money for him. Is that it? I don't mind paying you something. How about five dollars?"

Don shook his head.

"Six dollars?"

"I don't want to sell him," said Don.

They walked back to the house. Father came out.

"Did you two make a deal?" he asked.

"Your boy doesn't want to sell," said Mr. Holt.

"*Sell*?" said Father. "I thought you

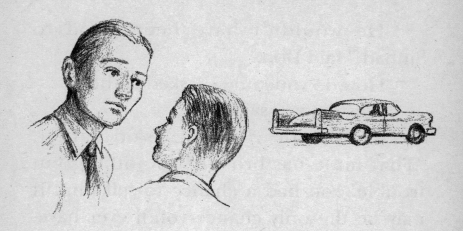

wanted to *give* the mule away."

"I did," said Don, "only—"

"I'll give you ten dollars," said Mr. Holt. "What do you say?"

"No," said Don.

"I think you'll be sorry," said Mr. Holt. He got into his car and drove away.

Father said, "He wanted to *buy* the mule. He wanted to give you ten dollars, and you wouldn't sell!"

"Not to him," said Don.

"Why not to him?" asked Father.

"He wouldn't have been good to Sinbad," said Don.

"How do you know?" asked Father.

"I just know," said Don.

"That's not a reason," said Father. "That mule has brought us nothing but trouble. You had a chance to sell him. It may be the only chance you'll ever have, and you didn't take it. I don't understand it. I don't understand *you*."

He started into the house. He stopped and turned around. "I thought you were ready for a horse of your own—the best horse we could buy for you. But now I see you'd rather have a mule!"

And he went on into the house.

10. Thanksgiving Day

Thanksgiving Day was sunny and bright.

Mother said, "It's the warmest Thanksgiving I can remember."

They had dinner by the fireplace. They did not need the fire, but it was good to look at as they sat at the table. There were turkey and cranberries and sweet potatoes for dinner. There were little boiled onions and hot rolls with butter and plum jelly. There were pumpkin pies just out of the oven.

After dinner Don and Jenny went outside. They sat on the porch.

"You didn't eat much," she said.

"I wasn't very hungry," he said.

"It's still two days until your birthday," she said. "Maybe Father will change his mind about Ben Gold."

Don shook his head. "He says I'm not ready to have a horse. He means I can't have a horse as long as I have Sinbad."

"Even if you don't have Ben Gold on your birthday," she said, "maybe you can have him some day."

"I don't know how," said Don. "Jim Crane is ready to sell him. Someone will buy him any day now."

They said nothing for a while. Don looked at Jenny. She was drying her eyes.

"What are you crying for?" he asked.

"Because it's Thanksgiving," she said, "and nobody is happy."

But a little later something happened to make Jenny feel better. Mr. and Mrs. Hibbs sent their two granddaughters down to play with her.

The girls were Susan and Katherine Lee. Susan was Jenny's age. Katherine was two years older. They lived in the city, and they came to the Hibbs Ranch on holidays and vacations.

The girls swung one another in the swing. They made a playhouse in the yard.

When it was time for Susan and Katherine to go, their mother came for them.

"I saw your timber, and it's beautiful," said Mrs. Lee. "Couldn't we go up there on a picnic?"

"Yes," said Jenny, "and I know a wonderful place. It's up by a red rock cliff."

"Let's go, Mother," said Katherine. "You said we could have a picnic while we're on Thanksgiving vacation."

"It's a long walk," said Jenny, "but there's a good path."

"We like to walk," said Mrs. Lee. "If tomorrow is warm, we'll go. Can you go with us, Jenny?"

"Oh, yes!" said Jenny.

"You can be the guide," said Susan.

The next morning Mrs. Lee and Katherine and Susan stopped by for Jenny. The four of them started off, each with a picnic lunch.

Mother asked Don, "Why didn't you go?"

"Mrs. Lee didn't ask me," he said. "I didn't want to go, anyway. It's just for the girls."

"Your father is going to town to buy

chicken feed," said Mother. "Do you want to go with him?"

"No, I'll stay here," said Don.

He went to his room. On the wall was a picture of a horse. He had cut it out of a magazine because it looked like Ben Gold.

He took the picture down and put it out of sight under his bed.

He heard Father drive away to town. From the kitchen he heard the sound of music, and he knew that Mother was listening to the radio.

He tried to read a book, but he did not want to read. He kept going to the window and looking out. There was something strange about the day. The air was still. The sun shone through a mist.

Don went outside. He thought of taking some hay to Sinbad.

As he started to the barn, Mother called him. "I just heard some news on the radio," she said. "There's a cold wave on the way."

"Is that why the sky looks so strange?" asked Don.

"It may be," she said. "The cold is coming fast. It will be here before evening."

"Will it be very cold?" he asked.

"Yes, below freezing," she said, "and your father didn't wear a coat to town. But I'm not worried about him. He can drive home in a few minutes. I *am* worried about Jenny and the Lee girls and their mother. They didn't wear any warm clothes, and they won't know about the cold wave until it comes."

"I know where they went," said Don. "Shall I go tell them?"

"Oh, I wish you would," said Mother. "If you don't, I'm afraid they will have a cold walk home."

"I can get up there in a hurry," said Don. He was already on his way.

11. The Timber

A path led up through the timber. It ran along the river.

Following the path was a long walk to the red rock cliff.

Don knew a short cut. He had taken it before. It led down a high, steep bank.

He started down the bank. Faster and faster he went. He began to slide and could not stop himself.

A rock turned under his foot. He fell, and a sharp pain struck him in the leg. He rolled over and over. He stopped against a bush at the foot of the bank.

The pain in his leg made him shut his teeth tightly together. It was the leg he had broken last winter. He tried to move it. It would not move. He was sure the leg was broken again.

He lay still, trying to think. The path was a mile away. He could not hope to walk there.

He sat up and began to call for help. He called again and again, and listened for an answer. But there was no answer. He had not thought there would be. Few people came to this part of the timber.

He lay down again. His leg did not hurt quite so much now. It was growing numb.

A wind sprang up and quickly died. Don felt a chill in the air.

For a little while he had forgotten why he had come here. Now he remembered. He had come to tell Jenny and her friends that a cold wave was on the way.

"Freezing before evening," Mother had said.

He began to shout again, "Help— help!"

He shouted until he was hoarse. Still there was no answer.

The sun had gone down. The cold had come. Don could feel it through his jeans and his thin sweater.

He knew that someone would be looking for him soon. But the timber was big. He was far from the path. How long would it be before anyone found him?

He listened. He was sure he heard footsteps. They were coming toward him. He saw something dark moving through the timber.

"Here!" he called. "Over here!"

Then, in spite of the pain and cold, he began to laugh.

"Sinbad!" he said.

The mule came close to him.

"Good old Sinbad—*you* heard me!" said Don. "Sinbad, help me out of here."

He stood up on one foot. But, even before he tried, he knew he could not climb onto the mule's back.

Sinbad flapped his ears and tried to lean against him.

"No," said Don, "This time I have to lean on you."

He was glad the mule was here. Now he would not be alone. And he was glad for another reason. Sinbad was warm.

He stood on one foot, with his arms over the mule's back. Whenever Sinbad moved, Don was afraid he might walk away.

"Don't go," he kept saying.

Night came, with stars and a bright
moon. Frost sparkled on the trees and
bushes. Don's arms and legs were numb.
Slowly he slid to the ground.

Sinbad touched him with his nose.

"Lie down," said Don. He lifted himself
as close as he could to Sinbad's ear. He
whispered, "Lie down—lie down!" and he

pulled at Sinbad's head.

At first the mule did not move. Then, slowly, he bent his front legs. He was lying down!

Don lay close to him. He could still feel the cold, but he could feel the warmth of Sinbad's body, too.

The night was long. Don could not sleep or rest. Sometimes the pain in his leg was dull, sometimes it was sharp.

With the first light of day, Sinbad moved.

"Don't go," said Don. "Wait!"

But Sinbad got to his feet. He lifted his head and brayed: "E-e-e-onk—e-e-e-onk—onk, onk!"

Don tried to get up, but he was too weak and too stiff with cold.

"Come back, Sinbad," he said. "I'll freeze if you go away!"

There were dead leaves on the ground.

He began to cover himself with them. While he was raking more leaves up about him, he saw a light through the trees. He heard footsteps.

A voice spoke: "That mule wasn't far off. If he and Don are together, they ought to be right here."

It was Mr. Hibbs' voice.

"Here!" shouted Don.

Lantern light flashed in his eyes. He heard his father say, "Don!" and he felt his father's arms around him.

12. *Through the Window*

Father told Don afterward, "You'd had about all you could stand that morning. You didn't know where you were when we took you out of the timber. You kept saying, 'Turn on the light.' Do you remember?"

Don did not remember. He remembered very little until the next morning and he was lying in his own bed. There was a pillow behind him. He could see a long, white cast on his leg.

His mother and father and Jenny were in the room.

Mother said, "How do you feel?"

He said, "I'm all right. Could I get up?"

"No, and you can't go to school for a while," said Father, "but you can study at home."

"I'll get your books when I go to school Monday," said Jenny.

Don asked her, "What about the picnic? Did you get home before the cold wave?"

"No," she said. "It got colder and colder up at the red rock cliff. It got so cold, we came home early. We ran to keep warm."

"When *was* the picnic?" he asked. "What day is this?"

"This is Sunday," said Mother. "It's the day after your birthday."

"But you can have your birthday today," said Jenny.

"Yes, if you feel like it," Mother told him. "You slept yesterday, and we thought you'd feel more like having your presents today."

"I'll bring the presents!" Jenny ran out and brought in some packages. She put them on the bed.

Don opened them. "Here's that basketball I wanted," he said. And, "A pair of skates! I won't try them today, though!" And, "A hunting cap! I wish I'd had this in the timber to keep my ears warm."

Father went outside.

"Shut your eyes," said Jenny.

Don shut his eyes.

"Keep them shut," she said.

He waited. "It's taking a long time."

"Now!" said Jenny.

He opened his eyes.

Mother and Jenny were looking out the window. He looked out the window, too.

Father had just come into the yard. He was leading a horse—a slim, bay horse with golden mane.

"Ben Gold!" said Don.

Father led him up to the window.

Don asked Mother, "Is he—is he going to be mine?"

She nodded.

"I thought—" Don stopped for a moment. "I thought I couldn't have a horse as long as I kept Sinbad. Is Sinbad gone?"

"If you'll look, you can see him," said Mother.

He looked past Father and Ben Gold. In the barn, with his head out the doorway of the box stall, was Sinbad.

"Your father has changed his mind about some things," said Mother. "He thinks Sinbad may have saved your life."

"And Sinbad and Ben Gold like each other," said Jenny. "Father was afraid a mule and a horse might fight, but they didn't. They're going to be friends."

Don sat looking out the window. "Look at Ben Gold—the way he stands—like a show horse. Isn't he beautiful?" Then he said, "Look at old Sinbad with his tongue hanging out. He's kind of beautiful, too!"